Charlie Thomas

I celebrated World Book Day 2019
with this brilliant gift from my local
Bookseller and Puffin Books.

CELEBRATE STORIES. LOVE READING.

This book has been specially published to celebrate **World Book Day**. We are a charity who offers every child and young person the opportunity to read and love books by giving you the chance to have a book of your own. To find out more, and for oodles of fun activities and reading recommendations to continue your reading journey, visit **worldbookday.com**

World Book Day in the UK and Ireland is made possible by generous sponsorship from National Book Tokens, participating publishers, booksellers, authors and illustrators. The £1* book tokens are a gift from your local bookseller.

World Book Day works in partnership with a number of charities, all of whom are working to encourage a love of reading for pleasure.

The National Literacy Trust is an independent charity that encourages children and young people to enjoy reading. Just 10 minutes of reading every day can make a big difference to how well you do at school and to how successful you could be in life. **literacytrust.org.uk**

The Reading Agency inspires people of all ages and backgrounds to read for pleasure and empowerment. They run the Summer Reading Challenge in partnership with libraries; they also support reading groups in schools and libraries all year round. Find out more and join your local library. **summerreadingchallenge.org.uk**

World Book Day also facilitates fundraising for:

Book Aid International, an international book donation and library development charity. Every year, they provide one million books to libraries and schools in communities where children would otherwise have little or no opportunity to read. **bookaid.org**

Read for Good, who motivate children in schools to read for fun through its sponsored read, which thousands of schools run on World Book Day and throughout the year. The money raised provides new books and resident storytellers in all the children's hospitals in the UK. **readforgood.org**

* €1.50 in Ireland

PUFFIN BOOKS

UK | USA | Canada | Ireland | Australia
India | New Zealand | South Africa

Puffin Books is part of the Penguin Random House group of companies
whose addresses can be found at global.penguinrandomhouse.com.

www.penguin.co.uk   www.puffin.co.uk   www.ladybird.co.uk

First published in the USA by HarperCollins Children's Books in *Guys Read: Other Worlds* 2013
Published in Great Britain as an ebook 2018
This edition published for World Book Day 2019

001

Text copyright © Rick Riordan, 2013
Puzzles and guides first published in *The Demigod Diaries*;
text copyright © Rick Riordan, 2009
Cover illustration copyright © Maximilian Meinzold, 2019

Little Badman and the Invasion of the Killer Aunties extract:
Written by Humza Arshad and Henry White
Text copyright © Big Deal Films Ltd, 2019
Illustrations copyright © Aleksei Bitskoff, 2019

The moral right of the authors and illustrator has been asserted

A CIP catalogue record for this book is available from the British Library

ISBN: 978-0-241-38073-4

All correspondence to:
Puffin Books, Penguin Random House Children's
80 Strand, London WC2R 0RL

PERCY
JACKSON
AND THE
SINGER OF APOLLO

RICK
RIORDAN

PUFFIN

Books by Rick Riordan

www.rickriordan.co.uk

* Also available as a graphic novel

Contents

I

I know what you're going to ask.

'Percy Jackson, why are you hanging from a Times Square billboard without your jeans on, about to fall to your death?'

Good question. You can blame Apollo, god of music, archery and poetry – also the god of making me do stupid quests.

This particular disaster started when I brought my friend Grover some aluminium cans for his birthday.

Perhaps I should mention . . . I'm a demigod. My dad, Poseidon, is the lord of the sea, which sounds cool, I guess, but mostly it means my life is filled with monster attacks and annoying Greek gods who tend to pop up on the subway or in the middle of maths class or when I'm taking a shower. (Long story. Don't ask.)

I figured maybe I'd get a day off from the craziness for Grover's birthday, but of course I was wrong.

Grover and his girlfriend, Juniper, were spending the day in Prospect Park in Brooklyn, doing naturey stuff like dancing with the local tree nymphs and serenading the squirrels. Grover's a satyr. That's his idea of fun.

Juniper seemed to be having an especially good time. While Grover and I sat on the bench together, she frolicked across Long Meadow with the other nature spirits, her chlorophyll-tinted eyes glinting in the sunlight. Since she was a dryad, Juniper's life source was tied to a juniper bush back on Long Island, but Grover explained that she could take short trips away from home as long as she kept a handful of fresh juniper berries in her pockets. I didn't want to ask what would happen if the berries got accidentally smashed.

Anyway, we hung out for a while, talking and enjoying the nice weather. I gave Grover his aluminium cans, which may sound like a lame gift, but that's his favourite snack.

He happily munched on the cans while the nymphs started discussing what party games we should play. Grover pulled a blindfold out of his pocket and suggested Pin the Tail on the Human, which made me kind of nervous since I was the only human.

Then, without warning, the sunlight brightened. The air turned uncomfortably hot. Twenty feet away, the grass hissed and a cloud of steam whooshed up like somebody had opened a big pressing machine at a laundromat. The steam cleared, and standing in front of us was the god Apollo.

Gods can look like anything they want, but Apollo always seemed to go for that I-just-auditioned-for-a-boy-band look. Today he was rocking pencil-thin jeans, a skintight white T-shirt and gilded Ray-Ban sunglasses. His wavy blond hair glistened with product. When he smiled the dryads squealed and giggled.

'Oh, no . . .' Grover murmured. 'This can't be good.'

'Percy Jackson!' Apollo beamed at me. 'And, um, your goat friend –'

'His name is Grover,' I said. 'And we're kind of off duty, Lord Apollo. It's Grover's birthday.'

'Happy birthday!' Apollo said. 'I'm so glad you're taking the day off. That means you two have time to help me with a small problem!'

2

Naturally, the problem wasn't small.

Apollo led Grover and me away from the party so we could talk in private. Juniper didn't want to let Grover go, but she couldn't argue with a god. Grover promised to come back safely. I hoped it was a promise he'd be able to keep.

When we got to the edge of the woods, Apollo faced us. 'Allow me to introduce the chryseae celedones.'

The god snapped his fingers. More steam erupted from the ground and three golden women appeared in front of us. When I say golden, I mean they were literally gold. Their metallic skin glittered. Their sleeveless gowns were made from enough gilded fabric to finance a bailout. Their golden hair was braided and piled on top of their heads in a sort of classical beehive hairdo. They were uniformly beautiful, and uniformly terrifying.

I'd seen living statues – automatons – many times before. Beautiful or not, they almost always tried to kill me.

'Uh . . .' I took a step back. 'What did you say these were? Krissy Kelly something?'

'Chryseae celedones,' Apollo said. 'Golden singers. They're my backup band!'

I glanced at Grover, wondering if this was some kind of joke.

Grover wasn't laughing. His mouth hung open in amazement, as if the golden ladies were the largest, tastiest aluminium cans he'd ever seen. 'I – I didn't think they were real!'

Apollo smiled. 'Well, it's been a few centuries since I brought them out. If they perform too often, you know, their novelty wears off. They used to live at my temple in Delphi. Man, they could rock that place. Now I only use them for special occasions.'

Grover got teary-eyed. 'You brought them out for my birthday?'

Apollo laughed. 'No, fool! I've got a concert tonight on Mount Olympus. Everyone is going to be there! The Nine Muses are opening, and I'm performing a mix of old favourites and new material. I mean, it's not like I need the celedones. My solo career has been great. But people will expect to hear some of my classic hits with the girls: "Daphne on my Mind", "Stairway to Olympus", "Sweet Home Atlantis". It's going to be awesome!'

I tried not to look nauseous. I'd heard Apollo's poetry before and, if his music was even half that bad, this concert was going to blow harder than Aeolus the wind god.

'Great,' I said half-heartedly. 'So what's the problem?'

Apollo's smile faded. 'Listen.'

He turned to his golden singers and raised his hands like a conductor. On cue, they sang in harmony: '*Laaaa!*'

It was only one chord, but it filled me with bliss. I suddenly couldn't remember where I was or what I was doing. If the golden singers had decided to tear me to pieces at that moment, I wouldn't have resisted, as long as they kept singing. Nothing mattered to me except the sound.

Then the golden girls went silent. The feeling passed. Their faces returned to beautiful, impassive metal.

'That . . .' I swallowed. 'That was amazing.'

'Amazing?' Apollo wrinkled his nose. 'There are only three of them! Their harmonies sound empty. I can't perform without the full quartet.'

Grover was weeping with joy. 'They're so beautiful. They're perfect!'

I was kind of glad Juniper wasn't within earshot, since she's the jealous type.

Apollo crossed his tanned arms. 'They're not perfect, Mr Satyr. I need all four or the concert will be ruined. Unfortunately, my fourth celedon went rogue this morning. I can't find her anywhere.'

I looked at the three golden automatons staring at Apollo, quietly waiting for orders. 'Uh . . . how does a backup singer go rogue?'

Apollo made another conductor wave, and the singers sighed in three-part harmony. The sound was so mournful my heart sank into my gut. At that moment I felt sure I'd never be happy again. Then, just as quickly, the feeling dissipated.

'They're out of warranty,' the god explained. 'Hephaestus made them for me back in the old days, and they worked fine . . . until the day after their two-thousand-year warranty expired. Then, naturally, *WHAM!* The fourth one goes haywire and runs off to the big city.' He gestured in the general direction of Manhattan. 'Of course I tried to complain to Hephaestus, but he's all, "Well, did you have my Protection Plus package?" And I'm like, "I didn't want your stupid extended warranty!" And he acts as if it's my fault the celedon broke, and says if I'd bought the Plus package I could've had a dedicated service hotline, but –'

'Whoa, whoa, whoa,' I interrupted. I really didn't want to get in the middle of a god-versus-god argument. I'd been there too many times. 'So if you know that your celedon is in the city, why can't you just look for her yourself?'

'I don't have time! I have to practise. I have to write a set list and do a sound check! Besides, this is what heroes are for.'

'Running the gods' errands,' I muttered.

'Exactly.' Apollo spread his hands. 'I assume the

missing celedon is roaming the Theater District, looking for a suitable place to audition. Celedones have the usual starlet dreams – being discovered, headlining a Broadway musical, that sort of thing. Most of the time I can keep their ambitions under control. I mean, I can't have them upstaging me, can I? But I'm sure without me around she thinks she's the next Katy Perry. You two need to get her before she causes any problems. And hurry! The concert is tonight and Manhattan is a large island.'

Grover tugged his goatee. 'So . . . you want us to find her, while you do sound checks?'

'Think of it as a favour,' Apollo said. 'Not just for me but for all those mortals in Manhattan.'

'Oh.' Grover's voice got very small. 'Oh, no . . .'

'What?' I demanded. 'What *oh, no?*'

Years ago, Grover created a magic empathy link between us (another long story) and we could sense each other's emotions. It wasn't exactly mind reading, but I could tell he was terrified.

'Percy,' he said, 'if that celedon starts singing in public, in the middle of afternoon rush hour –'

'She'll cause no end of havoc,' Apollo said. 'She might

sing a love song or a lullaby or a patriotic war tune, and whatever the mortals hear . . .'

I shuddered. One sigh from the golden girls had plunged me into despair, even with Apollo controlling their power. I imagined a rogue celedon bursting into song in a crowded city – putting people to sleep, or making them fall in love, or urging them to fight.

'She has to be stopped,' I agreed. 'But why us?'

'I like you!' Apollo grinned. 'You've faced the Sirens before. This isn't too different. Just put some wax in your ears. Besides, your friend Grover here is a satyr. He has natural resistance to magical music. Plus he can play the lyre.'

'What lyre?' I asked.

Apollo snapped his fingers. Suddenly Grover was holding the weirdest musical instrument I'd ever seen. The base was a hollowed-out tortoise shell, which made me feel really bad for the tortoise. Two polished wooden arms stuck out of one side like a bull's horns, with a bar across the top and seven strings stretching from the bar to the base of the shell. It looked like a combination harp, banjo and dead turtle.

'Oh!' Grover almost dropped the lyre. 'I couldn't! This is your –'

'Yes,' Apollo agreed cheerfully. 'That's my own personal lyre. Of course, if you damage it, I'll incinerate you, but I'm sure you'll be careful! You *can* play the lyre, can't you?'

'Um . . .' Grover plucked a few notes that sounded like a funeral dirge.

'Keep practising,' Apollo said. 'You'll need the lyre's magic to capture the celedon. Have Percy distract her while you play.'

'Distract her,' I repeated.

This quest was sounding worse and worse. I didn't see how a tortoiseshell harp could defeat a golden automaton, but Apollo clapped me on the shoulder like everything was settled.

'Excellent!' he said. 'I'll meet you at the Empire State Building at sunset. Bring me the celedon. One way or another I'll persuade Hephaestus to fix her. Just don't be late! I can't keep my audience waiting. And remember – not a scratch on that lyre.'

Then the sun god and his golden backup singers disappeared in a cloud of steam.

'Happy birthday to me,' Grover whimpered, and plucked a sour note on the harp.

3

We caught the subway to Times Square. We figured that would be a good place to start looking. It was in the middle of the Theater District and full of weird street performers and about a billion tourists, so it was the natural place for a golden diva to get some attention for herself.

Grover hadn't bothered disguising himself. His white T-shirt read WHAT WOULD PAN DO? The tips of his horns stuck out from his curly hair. Usually he wore jeans over his shaggy legs and specially fitted shoes over his hooves, but today from the waist down he was *au naturel* goat.

I doubted it would matter. Most mortals couldn't see

through the Mist, which hid the true appearance of monsters. Even without Grover's normal disguise, people would have to look really closely to notice he was a satyr, and even then they probably wouldn't bat an eye. This was New York, after all.

As we pushed through the crowd, I kept searching for the glint of gold, hoping to spot the rogue celedon, but the square was packed as usual. A guy wearing only his underwear and a guitar was having his picture taken with some tourists. Cops hung out on the street corners, looking bored. At Broadway and West Forty-Ninth, the intersection was blocked and a crew of roadies was setting up some sort of stage. Preachers, ticket touts and hawkers shouted over each other, trying to get attention. Music blasted from dozens of loudspeakers, but I didn't hear any magical singing.

Grover had given me a ball of warm wax to stuff in my ears whenever necessary. He said he always kept some handy, like chewing gum, which didn't make me anxious to use it.

He bumped into a pretzel vendor's cart and lurched back, hugging Apollo's lyre protectively.

'You know how to use that thing?' I asked. 'I mean, what kind of magic does it do?'

Grover's eyes widened. 'You don't know? Apollo built the walls of Troy just by playing this harp. With the right song, it can create almost anything!'

'Like a cage for the celedon?' I asked.

'Uh . . . yeah!'

He didn't sound too confident, and I wasn't sure I wanted him playing *Guitar Hero* with a godly tortoise banjo. Sure, Grover could do some magic with his reed pipes. On a good day he could make plants grow and entangle his enemies. On a bad day he could only remember Justin Bieber songs, which didn't do anything except give me a headache.

I tried to think of a plan. I wished my girlfriend, Annabeth, was here. She was more of the planning type. Unfortunately, she was off in San Francisco visiting her dad.

Grover grabbed my arm. 'There.'

I followed his gaze. Across the square, at the outdoor stage, workers scurried around, installing lights on the scaffolding, setting up microphone stands and plugging in giant speakers. Probably they were prepping for a Broadway musical preview or something.

Then I saw her — a golden lady making her way towards the platform. She climbed over the police barricades that cordoned off the intersection, squeezed between workers who completely ignored her and headed for the steps, stage right. She glanced at the crowd in Times Square and smiled, as if imagining their wild applause. Then she headed for the centre microphone.

'Oh, gods!' Grover yelped. 'If that sound system is on . . .'

I stuffed wax in my ears as we ran for the stage.

4

Fighting automatons is bad enough. Fighting one in a crowd of mortals is a recipe for disaster. I didn't want to worry about the mortals' safety *and* mine *and* figure out how to capture the celedon. I needed a way to evacuate Times Square without causing a stampede.

As we weaved through the crowd, I grabbed the nearest cop by the shoulder.

'Hey!' I told him. 'Presidential motorcade coming! You guys better clear the streets!'

I pointed down Seventh Avenue. Of course there was no motorcade, but I did my best to imagine one.

See, some demigods can actually control the Mist. They can make people see what they want them to see. I wasn't very good at it, but it was worth a shot. Presidential visits are common enough, with the United Nations in town and all, so I figured the cop might buy it.

Apparently he did. He glanced towards my imaginary line of limos, made a disgusted face and said something into his two-way radio. With the wax in my ears, I couldn't hear what, but all the other cops in the square started herding the crowd towards the side streets.

Unfortunately, the celedon had reached centre stage.

We were still fifty feet away when she grabbed the mike and tapped it. *BOOM, BOOM, BOOM* echoed through the streets.

'Grover,' I yelled, 'you'd better start playing that lyre.'

If he responded, I didn't hear it. I sprinted for the stage. The workers were too busy arguing with the cops to try stopping me. I bounded up the steps, pulled my pen out of my pocket and uncapped it. My sword, Riptide, sprang into existence, though I wasn't sure it would help me. Apollo wouldn't be happy with me if I decapitated his backup singer.

I was twenty feet from the celedon when a lot of things happened at once.

The golden singer belted out a note so powerful I could hear it through the wax plugs. Her voice was heartbreakingly sad, filled with longing. Even muffled through the wax, it made me want to break down and cry – which is what several thousand people around Times Square did. Cars stopped. Police and tourists fell to their knees, weeping, hugging each other in consolation.

Then I became aware of a different sound – Grover, frantically strumming his lyre. I couldn't exactly hear it, but I could feel the tremor of magic rippling through the air, shaking the stage under my feet. Thanks to the empathy link, I caught flashes of Grover's thoughts. He was singing about walls, trying to summon a box around the celedon.

The good news: it sort of worked. A brick wall erupted from the stage between me and the celedon, knocking over the mike stand and interrupting her song. The bad news: by the time I'd figured out what was going on, I couldn't stop my momentum. I ran straight into the wall, which wasn't mortared, so I promptly collapsed on top of the celedon, along with about a thousand bricks.

My eyes watered. My nose felt broken. Before I could regain my bearings, the celedon struggled out of the pile of bricks and pushed me off. She raised her arms in triumph, as if the whole thing had been a planned stunt.

She sang, '*Ta-daaaaah!*'

She was no longer amplified, but her voice carried. The mortals stopped sobbing and rose to their feet, clapping and cheering for the celedon.

'Grover!' I yelled, not sure if he could hear me. 'Play something else!'

I picked up my sword and struggled to my feet. I tackled the golden lady, but it was like tackling a lamp post. She ignored me and launched into song.

As I wrestled with her, trying to pull her off balance, the temperature on stage began to rise. The celedon's lyrics were in Ancient Greek, but I caught a few of the words: *Apollo, sunlight, golden fire.* It was some kind of ode to the god. Her metal skin grew hot. I smelled something burning and realized it was my shirt.

I stumbled away from her, my clothes smouldering. The wax had melted out of my ears so I could hear her song clearly. All around Times Square, people started dropping from the heat.

Over at the barricades, Grover played wildly on the lyre, but he was too anxious to focus. Random bricks fell from the sky. One of the monitor speakers on stage morphed into a chicken. A plate of enchiladas appeared at the celedon's feet.

'Not helpful!' I shouted through the pain of the rising heat. 'Sing about cages! Or gags!'

The air felt like a blast furnace. If the celedon kept this up, Midtown would burst into flames. I couldn't afford to play nice any more. As the celedon started her next verse, I lunged at her with my sword.

She lurched away with surprising speed. The tip of my blade missed her face by an inch. I'd managed to stop her singing, and she was not happy about it. She glared at me in outrage, then focused on my blade. Fear flickered across her metallic face. Most magical beings knew enough to respect Celestial bronze, since it could vaporize them on contact.

'Surrender and I won't hurt you,' I said. 'We just want to take you back to Apollo.'

She spread her arms. I was afraid she was going to sing again, but instead the celedon changed form. Her arms grew into golden feathery wings. Her face elongated, growing a beak. Her body shrank until I was staring at a plump metal bird about the size of a quail. Before I could react, the celedon launched herself into the air and flew straight for the top of the nearest building.

Grover stumbled onto the stage next to me. All across Times Square, the mortals who had collapsed from the heat were starting to recover. The pavement still steamed. Police started shouting orders, making a serious effort now to clear the area. Nobody paid us any attention.

I watched the golden bird spiral up until she disappeared over the highest billboard on the Times Tower. You've probably seen the building in pictures: the tall skinny one that's stacked with glowing advertisements and jumbotron screens.

To be completely honest, I didn't feel so great. I had hot wax melting out of my ears. I'd been chargrilled medium rare. My face felt like it had just been rammed into a brick wall . . . because it had. I had the coppery taste of blood in my mouth, and I was really starting to hate music. And quails.

I turned to Grover. 'Did you know she could morph into a bird?'

'Uh, yeah . . . But I kind of forgot.'

'Great.' I nudged the enchilada plate at my feet. 'Could you try to summon something more helpful next time?'

'Sorry,' he murmured. 'I get hungry when I get nervous. So what do we do now?'

I stared up at the top of the Times Tower. 'The golden girl wins round one. Time for round two.'

5

You're probably wondering why I didn't put more wax in my ears. For one thing, I didn't have any. For another thing, wax melting out of my ears hurts. And maybe part of me was thinking: *Hey, I'm a demigod. This time I'm prepared. I can face the music, literally.*

Grover assured me he had the lyre figured out. No more enchiladas or bricks falling from the sky. I just had to find the celedon, catch her by surprise and distract her by . . . well, I hadn't figured out that part yet.

We took the elevator to the top floor of the Times Tower and found stairs to the roof. I wished I could fly, but that wasn't one of my powers, and my pegasus friend Blackjack hadn't been answering my calls for help lately.

(He gets a little distracted in the springtime when he's searching the skies for cute lady pegasi.)

Once we made it to the roof, the celedon was easy to find. She was in human form, standing at the edge of the building with her arms spread, serenading Times Square with her own rendition of 'New York, New York'.

I really hate that song. I don't know anybody who's actually from New York who doesn't hate that song, but hearing her sing it made me hate it a whole lot more.

Anyway, she had her back to us, so we had an advantage. I was tempted to sneak up behind her and push her off, but she was so strong I hadn't been able to budge her before. Besides, she'd probably just turn into a bird and . . . Hmm. A bird.

An idea formed in my mind. Yes, I *do* get ideas sometimes.

'Grover,' I said, 'can you use the lyre to summon a birdcage? Like, a really strong one, made of Celestial bronze?'

He pursed his lips. 'I suppose, but birds shouldn't be caged, Percy. They should be free! They should fly and –' He looked at the celedon. 'Oh, you mean –'

'Yeah.'

'I'll try.'

'Good,' I said. 'Just wait for my cue. Do you still have that blindfold from Pin the Tail on the Human?'

He handed me the strip of cloth. I shrank my sword to ballpoint-pen form and slipped it in the pocket of my jeans. I'd need both hands free for this. I crept up on the celedon, who was now belting out the final chorus.

Even though she was facing the other way, her music filled me with the urge to dance (which, believe me, you never want to see). I forced myself to keep going, but fighting her magic was like pushing my way through a row of heavy drapes.

My plan was simple: gag the celedon. She would turn back into a bird and try to escape. I would grab her and shove her into a birdcage. What could go wrong?

On the last line of 'New York, New York' I jumped on her back, locking my legs around her waist and yanking the blindfold across her mouth like a bit on a horse's bridle.

Her grand finale was cut short with a 'New Yor— *urff!*'

'Grover, now!' I yelled.

The celedon stumbled forward. I had a dizzying view of the chaos below in Times Square — cops trying to clear the crowd, lines of tourists doing impromptu high-kick routines like the Radio City Rockettes. The electronic billboards down the side of the Times Tower looked like a very steep, psychedelic waterslide, with nothing but hard pavement at the bottom.

The celedon staggered backwards, flailing and mumbling through the gag.

Grover desperately strummed his lyre. The strings sent powerful magic vibrations through the air, but Grover's voice quivered with uncertainty.

'Um, birds!' he warbled. 'La, la, la! Birds in cages! Very strong cages! Birds!'

He wasn't going to win any Grammys with those lyrics, and I was losing my grip. The celedon was strong. I'd ridden the Minotaur before, and the golden lady was at least that hard to hold on to.

The celedon spun around, trying to throw me. She clamped her hands onto my forearms and squeezed. Pain shot up to my shoulders.

I yelled, 'Grover, hurry!' But, with my teeth clenched, the words came out more like, '*Grr – huh.*'

'Birds in cages!' Grover strummed another chord. 'La, la, la, cages!'

Amazingly, a birdcage shimmered into being at the edge of the roof. I was too busy getting tossed around to have a proper look, but Grover seemed to have done a good job. The cage was just large enough for a parrot or a fat quail, and the bars glowed faintly . . . Celestial bronze.

Now, if I could just get the celedon into bird form. Unfortunately, she wasn't cooperating. She spun around hard, breaking my grip and shoving me over the side of the building.

I tried not to panic. Sadly, this wasn't the first time I'd been thrown off a skyscraper.

I'd like to tell you that I did some cool acrobatic move, grabbed the edge of a billboard and vaulted back up to the roof in a perfect triple flip.

Nope. As I bounced off the first jumbotron screen, a metal strut somehow snagged my belt and stopped me from falling. It also gave me the ultimate wedgie of all time. Then, as if that wasn't bad enough, my momentum spun me upside down and I peeled right out of my jeans.

I plummeted head first towards Times Square, grabbing wildly for anything to slow me down. Luckily, the top of the next billboard had a rung across it, maybe for extremely brave maintenance workers to latch their harnesses on to.

I managed to catch it and flipped right side up. My arms were nearly yanked out of their sockets, but somehow I kept my grip. And that's how I ended up hanging from a billboard over Times Square without my jeans.

To answer your next question: boxers. Plain blue boxers. No smiley faces. No hearts.

Laugh all you want. They're more comfortable than briefs.

The celedon smiled at me from the top of the roof, about twenty feet above. Just below her, my jeans hung from the metal strut, blowing in the wind like they were waving me goodbye. I couldn't see Grover. His music had stopped.

My grip weakened. The pavement was maybe seven hundred feet down, which would make for a very long scream as I fell to my death. The glowing screen of the jumbotron was slowly cooking my stomach.

As I was dangling there, the celedon began a special serenade just for me. She sang about letting go, laying down my troubles, resting by the banks of a river. I don't remember the exact lyrics, but you get the idea.

It was all I could do to hold on. I didn't want to drop, but the celedon's music washed over me, dismantling my resolve. I imagined myself floating down safely. I would land on the banks of a lazy river, where I could have a nice relaxing picnic with my girlfriend.

Annabeth.

I remembered the time I'd saved Annabeth from the Sirens in the Sea of Monsters. I'd held her while she cried and struggled, trying to swim to her death because she thought she would reach some beautiful promised land.

Now I imagined she was holding me back. I could hear what she'd say: *It's a trick, Seaweed Brain! You've got to trick her back or you'll die. And if you die I'll never forgive you!*

That broke the celedon's spell. Annabeth's anger was way scarier than most monsters, but don't tell her I said that.

I looked up at my jeans, dangling uselessly above. My sword was in pen form in the pocket, where it did me no good. Grover had started to sing about birds again, but it wasn't helping. Apparently the celedon only turned into bird form when she was startled.

Wait . . .

Out of desperation, I formed Stupid Plan Version 2.0.

'Hey!' I called up. 'You really are amazing, Miss Celedon! Before I die, can I have your autograph?'

The celedon halted mid-song. She looked surprised, then smiled with pleasure.

'Grover!' I called. 'Come over here!'

The lyre music stopped. Grover's head poked over the side. 'Oh, Percy . . . I – I'm sorry –'

'It's okay!' I faked a smile, using our empathy link to tell him how I really felt. I couldn't send complete thoughts, but I tried to get the general point across: he needed to be ready; he needed to be quick. I hoped he was good at catching.

'Do you have a pen and paper?' I asked him. 'I want to get this lady's autograph before I die.'

Grover blinked. 'Uh . . . jeez. No. But isn't there a pen

in the pocket of your jeans?'

Best. Satyr. Ever. He totally got the plan.

'You're right!' I gazed up at the celedon imploringly. 'Please? Last request? Could you just fish the pen out of my jeans and sign them? Then I can die happy.'

Golden statues can't blush, but the celedon looked extremely flattered. She reached down, retrieved my jeans and pulled out the pen.

I caught my breath. I'd never seen Riptide in the hands of a monster before. If this went wrong, if she realized it was a trick, she could kill Grover. Celestial bronze blades work just fine on satyrs.

She examined the pen like she'd never used one before.

'You have to take the cap off,' I said helpfully. My fingers were beginning to slip.

She laid the jeans on the ledge, next to the birdcage. She uncapped the pen and Riptide sprang to life.

If I hadn't been about to die, it would've been the funniest thing I'd ever seen. You know those trick cans of candy with the coiled-up toy snake inside? It was like watching somebody open one of those, except replace the toy snake with a three-foot-long blade.

The Celestial sword shot to full length and the celedon thrust it away, leaping backwards with a not-very-musical shriek. She turned into a bird, but Grover was ready. He dropped Apollo's lyre and caught the fat golden quail in both hands.

Grover stuffed her into the cage and slammed the door shut. The celedon went crazy, squawking and flapping, but she didn't have room to turn back into human form, and in bird form – thank the gods – she didn't seem to have any magic in her voice.

'Good job!' I called up to Grover.

He looked sick. 'I think I scratched Apollo's lyre. And I just caged a bird. This is the worst birthday ever.'

'By the way,' I reminded him, 'I'm about to fall to my death here.'

'Ah!' Grover snatched up the lyre and played a quick tune. Now that he wasn't in danger and the monster was caged, he seemed to have no problem using the harp's magic. Typical. He summoned a rope and threw it down to me. Somehow he managed to pull me to the top, where I collapsed.

Below us, Times Square was still in complete chaos.

Tourists wandered around in a daze. The cops were breaking up the last of the high-kick dance routines. A few cars were on fire, and the outdoor stage had been reduced to a pile of kindling, bricks and broken sound equipment.

Across the Hudson River, the sun was going down. All I wanted to do was lie there on the roof and enjoy the feeling of not being dead. But our job wasn't done yet.

'We've got to get the celedon back to Apollo,' I said.

'Yeah,' Grover agreed. 'But, uh . . . maybe put your jeans on first?'

6

Apollo was waiting for us in the lobby of the Empire State Building. His three golden singers paced nervously behind him.

When he saw us, he brightened – literally. A glowing aura appeared around his head.

'Excellent!' He took the birdcage. 'I'll get Hephaestus to fix her up, and this time I'm not taking any excuses about expired warranties. My show starts in half an hour!'

'You're welcome,' I said.

Apollo accepted the lyre from Grover. The god's expression turned dangerously stormy. 'You scratched it.'

Grover whimpered. 'Lord Apollo –'

'It was the only way to catch the celedon,' I interceded. 'Besides, it'll buff out. Get Hephaestus to do it. He owes you, right?'

For a second I thought Apollo might blast us both to ashes, but finally he just grunted. 'I suppose you're right. Well, good job, you two! As your reward, you're invited to watch me perform on Mount Olympus!'

Grover and I glanced at each other. Insulting a god was dangerous, but the last thing I wanted to do was hear more music.

'We aren't worthy,' I lied. 'We'd love to, really, but you know, we'd probably explode or something if we heard your godly music at full volume.'

Apollo nodded thoughtfully. 'You're right. It might distract from my performance if you exploded. How considerate of you.' He grinned. 'Well, I'm off, then. Happy birthday, Percy!'

'It's Grover's birthday,' I corrected, but Apollo and his singers had already disappeared in a flash of golden light.

'So much for a day off,' I said, turning back to Grover.

'Back to Prospect Park?' he suggested. 'Juniper must be worried to death.'

'Yeah,' I agreed. 'And I'm really hungry.'

Grover nodded enthusiastically. 'If we leave now, we can pick up Juniper and reach Camp Half-Blood in time for the sing-along. They have s'mores!'

I winced. 'No sing-along, please. But I'll go for the s'mores.'

'Deal!' Grover said.

I clapped him on the shoulder. 'Come on, G-man. Your birthday might turn out okay after all.'

WANT MORE FROM
THE WORLD OF

PERCY JACKSON?

TURN THE PAGE FOR PUZZLES,

A GUIDE TO THE GODS

AND A 'WHO'S WHO IN

GREEK MYTHOLOGY'

OLYMPIAN CROSSWORD PUZZLE

Test your knowledge of Percy Jackson
and the Olympians!

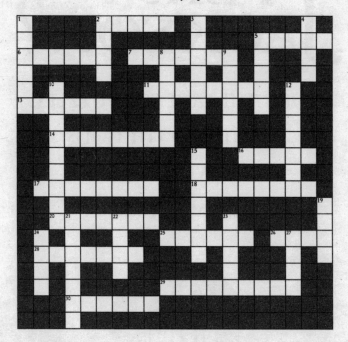

ACROSS

2. Lord of the Dead
5. The ____ Fates
6. Percy's best friend
7. Percy's half-brother Tyson is a ___
11. This monster wears Fruit of the Loom underwear
13. Percy's cousin, daughter of Zeus
14. Percy is entering this year at school (in *Percy Jackson and the Battle of the Labyrinth*)
16. Percy has the ability to control this element

17. God of the Sea
18. Hot-tempered female bully, daughter of Ares
20. Another name for a half-blood
25. Also known as 'The Kindly Ones'
26. Percy's mom loves food that is this colour
28. Percy's magical sword
29. Annabeth's hat makes her turn this
30. Luke is the son of this god

DOWN

1. Percy's birthday month
2. Wife of Zeus
3. Titan Lord
4. Lord of the Sky
5. Dr _____ (evil manticore in *Percy Jackson and the Titan's Curse*)
8. Activities Director at the camp
9. Medusa's hair is made of these
10. Camp visited by Percy and friends
12. Annabeth is deathly afraid of these creatures

15. Nike is the goddess of _____
19. Zeus's mother
21. Name of the link Percy and Grover share
22. Zeus, Poseidon and Hades are all ____.
23. Hydras have multiple ____
24. Thalia had once been turned into a _____
27. Aphrodite is the goddess of _____.

(Solution on page 48)

OLYMPIAN
WORD JUMBLE

Discover the hidden words lurking in this puzzle!

```
X N A M G I S P X K U P S I L K A M P E
R H O I C X H E P I T S N T A P P A K R
O Z E D H R E R T J A I A L A P H A T L I
S E R A I R B C K A M P T P U C X L A C
B T A E G E R Y O N B D I A H D N E F K
A A G D R H S I S U O J T I E I I D H R
C K L A O R H O L S D M R N L O H Y T I
K S P L V I N A P R O O N A L A P E N O
B N T U E O T Y S O N A R E H H S N I R
I A B S R T L P R Y I U X T O Z M U R D
T I E K A A N N A B E T H N U E C S Y A
E P T I C D E X C N S E F H N I C O B N
R M A N C R T O H E T A U X D R A N A P
H Y R I P T I D E A O M I C R O N I L A
O L M G A M M A L U K E O B I W A M E L
N O L I S P E Z E X I N C L A R I S S E
```

PERCY	KAMPÊ	MINOS
ANNABETH	CALYPSO	TITAN
TYSON	POSEIDON	OLYMPIANS
GROVER	JANUS	RICK RIORDAN (The Percy Author!)
DAEDALUS	KRONOS	
GERYON	PAN	
BRIARES	NICO	
CHIRON	LUKE	
HERA	LABYRINTH	
RACHEL	CLARISSE	
SPHINX	BACKBITER	
HELLHOUND	RIPTIDE	

(Solution on page 49)

CROSSWORD PUZZLE ANSWERS

(Solution to puzzle on page 44)

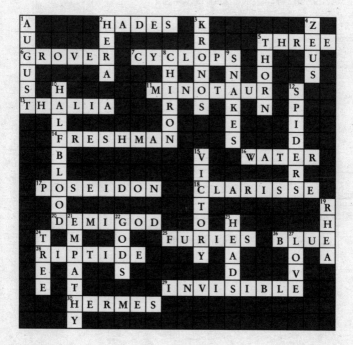

WORD JUMBLE ANSWERS

(Solution to puzzle on page 46)

```
X N A M G I S P X K U P S I L K A M P E
R H O I C X H E P I T S N T A P P A K R
O Z E D H R E R T J A I A L P H A T L I
S E R A I R B C K A M P T P U C X L A C
B T A E G E R Y O N B D I A H D N E F K
A A G D R H S I S U O J T I E I I D H R
C K L A O R H O L S D M R N L O H Y T I
K S P L V I N A P R O O N A L A P E N O
B N T U E O T Y S O N A R E H H S N I T
I A B S R T L P R Y I U X T O Z M U R D
T I E K A A N N A B E T H N U E C S Y A
E P T I C D E X C N S E F H N I C O B N
R M A N C R T O H E T A U X D R A N A P
H Y R I P T I D E A O M I C R O N I L A
O L M G A M M A L U K E O B I W A M E L
N O L I S P E Z E X I N C L A R I S S E
```

49

THE TWELVE OLYMPIAN
GODS PLUS TWO

A handy chart for all Olympians!

God / Goddess	Sphere of Control	animal / symbol
Zeus	sky	eagle, lightning bolt
Hera	motherhood, marriage	cow (motherly animal), lion, peacock
Poseidon	sea, earthquakes	horse, trident
Demeter	agriculture	red poppy, barley
Hephaestus	blacksmiths	anvil, quail (hops funnily, like him)
Athena	wisdom, battle, useful arts	owl
Aphrodite	love	dove, magic belt that makes men fall for her
Ares	war	wild boar, bloody spear

God / Goddess	Sphere of Control	animal / symbol
Apollo	music, medicine, poetry, archery, bachelors	mouse, lyre
Artemis	maiden girls, hunting	she-bear
Hermes	travellers, merchants, thieves, messengers	caduceus, winged helmet and sandals
Dionysus	wine	tiger, grapes
Hestia	home and hearth (gave up her council seat for Dionysus)	crane
Hades	the Underworld	helm of terror

PERCY JACKSON

A GUIDE TO
WHO'S
WHO
IN GREEK
MYTHOLOGY

ZEUS

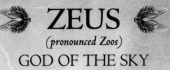

(pronounced Zoos)

GOD OF THE SKY

Distinguishing Features:

Pin-striped suit, neatly trimmed grey beard, stormy eyes and a very large, dangerous lightning bolt.

Now:

On stormy days, he can be found brooding in his throne room in Mount Olympus, over the Empire State Building in New York. Sometimes he travels the world in disguise, so be nice to everyone! You never know when the next person you meet might be packing the master bolt.

Then:

In the old days, Zeus ruled over his unruly family of Olympians while they bickered and fought and got jealous of each other. Not much different from today, really. Zeus always had an eye for beautiful women, which often got him in trouble with his wife, Hera. A less-than-stellar father figure, Zeus once tossed Hera's son Hephaestus off the top of Mount Olympus because the baby was too ugly!

POSEIDON

(Po-sy'-dun)

GOD OF THE SEA

Distinguishing Features:

Hawaiian shirt, shorts, flip-flops and a three-pointed trident.

Now:

Poseidon walks the beaches of Florida, occasionally stopping to chat with fishermen or take pictures for tourists. If he's in a bad mood, he stirs up a hurricane.

Then:

Poseidon was always a moody guy. On his good days, he did cool stuff like create horses out of sea foam. On his bad days, he caused minor problems like destroying cities with earthquakes or sinking entire fleets of ships. But, hey, a god has the right to throw a temper tantrum, doesn't he?

HADES

(Hay'-deez)

GOD OF THE UNDERWORLD

Distinguishing Features:

Evil smile, helm of darkness (which makes him invisible so you can't see the evil smile), black robes sewn from the souls of the damned. He sits on a throne of bones.

Now:

Hades rarely leaves his palace in the Underworld, probably because of traffic congestion on the Fields of Asphodel freeway. He oversees a booming population among the dead and has all sorts of employment trouble with his ghouls and spectres. This keeps him in a foul mood most of the time.

Then:

Hades is best known for the romantic way he won his wife, Persephone. He kidnapped her. Really, though, how would you like to marry someone who lives in a dark cave filled with zombies all year round?

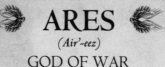

ARES

(Air'-eez)

GOD OF WAR

Distinguishing Features:

Biker leathers, Harley-Davidson, sunglasses and a stinking attitude.

Now:

Can be found riding his Harley around the suburbs of LA. One of those gods who could pick a fight in an empty room.

Then:

Back in the day, the son of Zeus and Hera used to be inseparable from his shield and helmet. Fought on the side of the Trojans during the war of Troy, but, frankly, has been involved in every minor skirmish since Goldilocks told the three bears that their beds were a little uncomfy.

❧ ATHENA ❧
(Ah-thee'-nah)
GODDESS OF WISDOM, WAR AND USEFUL ARTS

Distinguishing Features:
....

Dark hair, striking grey eyes, casual yet fashionable clothes, (except when she's going into battle; then it's full body armour). Athena is always accompanied by at least one owl, her sacred (and, fortunately, housebroken) animal.

Now:
....

You're likely to spot Athena at an American university, sitting in on lectures about military history or technology. She favours people who invent useful things, and will sometimes appear to reward them with magical gifts or bits of useful advice (like next week's lottery numbers). So start working on that revolutionary new bread slicer!

Then:
....

Athena was one of the most active goddesses in human affairs. She helped out Odysseus, sponsored the entire city of Athens and made sure the Greeks won the Trojan War. On the downside, she's proud and has a big temper. Just ask Arachne, who got turned into a spider for daring to compare her weaving skills to Athena's. So, whatever you do, DO NOT claim that you fix toilets better than Athena. There's no telling what she'll turn you into.

APHRODITE
(A-fro-dy'-tee)
GODDESS OF LOVE
AND BEAUTY

Distinguishing Features:

She's really, really pretty.

Now:

She's more beautiful than Angelina Jolie.

Then:

She was more beautiful than Helen of Troy and because of her beauty, other gods feared that jealousy would interrupt the peace between them and lead to war. Zeus was so frightened that she would be the cause of violence between the other gods that he married her off to Hephaestus. However, she was frequently unfaithful to her husband and it was even said that Aphrodite could make any man fall in love with her if they just laid eyes on her. Now that's power!

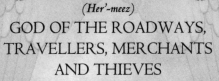

HERMES

(Her'-meez)

GOD OF THE ROADWAYS, TRAVELLERS, MERCHANTS AND THIEVES

Distinguishing Features:

Jogger's clothes and winged athletic shoes, a mobile phone that turns into a caduceus, his symbol of power – a winged staff with two snakes, George and Martha, entwined round it.

Now:

Hermes is a hard person to find because he's always on the run. When he's not delivering messages for the gods, he's running a telecommunications company, an express delivery service and every other type of business you can imagine that involves travel. Did you have a question about his activities as god of thieves? Leave a message. He'll get back to you in a few millennia.

Then:

Hermes got started young as a troublemaker. When he was one day old, he sneaked out of his crib and stole some cattle from his brother, Apollo. Apollo probably would've blasted the young tyke to bits, but fortunately Hermes appeased him with a new musical instrument he created called the lyre. Apollo liked it so much he forgot all about the cows. The lyre made Apollo very popular with the ladies, which was more than he could say about the cattle.

SIRENS

(Sy'-rens)

MONSTERS

Distinguishing Features:
....

Ugly bodies, faces like vultures, beautiful singing voices.
(Hey, that sounds like my elementary-school choir teacher . . .)

Now:
....

The Sirens inhabit the Sea of Monsters, where they lure
sailors to their deaths by singing sweet songs, something like
'80s Oldies radio, only worse.

Then:
....

Back in the day, the Sirens were a real threat to the Greek
shipping industry. Then a smart guy named Odysseus
discovered that you could plug your ears with wax
and sail right past the Sirens without hearing a thing.
Strangely, Odysseus is usually remembered for his other
accomplishments, not as the inventor of ear wax.

CIRCE

(Sear'-see)

ENCHANTRESS

Distinguishing Features:

Great hairdo, beautiful robes, enchanting singing voice, deadly wand hidden up her sleeve.

Now:

Circe runs a fashionable spa and resort on an island in the Sea of Monsters. Stop by if you'd like a makeover, but be warned: you might not leave the same person, or even the same species.

Then:

Circe loved to entertain sailors. She would welcome them warmly, feed them well, then turn them into pigs. Odysseus put a stop to this practice by eating a magic herb, then holding the sorceress at knife-point until she released his polymorphed crewmates. Circe promptly fell in love with Odysseus. Go figure.

DIONYSUS

(Dy-oh-ny'-sus)

GOD OF WINE

Distinguishing Features:

Leopard-skin shirt, walking shorts, purple socks and sandals, the general pasty demeanour of someone who has been up partying too late.

Now:

Dionysus has been sentenced to one hundred years of 'rehab' as director of Camp Half-Blood. The only thing the god of wine can drink these days is Diet Coke, which doesn't make him happy. He can usually be found playing pinochle with a group of terrified satyrs on the front porch of the Big House. If you want to join the game, be prepared to bet large.

Then:

Dionysus invented wine, which so impressed his father Zeus that he promoted Dionysus to god. The guy who invented prune juice, by contrast, got sentenced to the Fields of Punishment. Dionysus mostly spent his time partying it up in Ancient Greece, but once a crew of sailors tried to kill him, thinking the god was too incapacitated to fight back. Dionysus turned them into dolphins and sent them over the side. The moral of this story: do not mess with a god, even a drunk one.

POLYPHEMUS

(Poly-fee'-mus)

ELDER CYCLOPS

Distinguishing Features:

One large eye in the centre of his head, sheep breath, fashionable caveman outfit, bad dental hygiene.

Now:

The giant Polyphemus hangs out in a cave on a deserted island, where he herds sheep and enjoys simple pastoral pleasures, like eating the occasional Greek hero who happens to sail by.

Then:

The giant Polyphemus hung out in a cave on a deserted island, where he herded sheep and enjoyed simple pastoral pleasures, like eating the occasional Greek hero who happened to sail by. (Some monsters never learn.)

WANT TO JUMP INTO ANOTHER ADVENTURE?

You'll love this hilarious new book
from comedian Humza Arshad and
award-winning writer Henry White.

Turn the page for an extract . . .

Humza Khan is the greatest eleven-year-old rapper Eggington has ever known: he is Little Badman and soon everyone will know his name.

The problem is, school has got really weird: one by one, all the teachers are disappearing and suspicious aunties are taking over. It isn't so bad though – Humza can still record his first song and the aunties are very generous with snacks.

But when they start to mess with his music, Humza has to get to the bottom of what's going on. With the help of his friends Umer and Wendy, Humza must hunt for the truth. Can he stop the aunties before they carry out their evil plan?

LITTLE BADMAN

AND THE INVASION OF THE KILLER AUNTIES

Illustrated by
ALEKSEI BITSKOFF

HUMZA ARSHAD
& HENRY WHITE

HUMZA ARSHAD is the first British YouTuber to have his own scripted comedy series on BBC Three in the mockumentary series *Coconut*. Since accumulating over ninety million views on his channel, Humza has used his influence and comedy for a greater purpose. In 2015, Humza performed at one hundred and twenty schools using comedy to prevent at-risk teens from becoming radicalized. He is currently an ambassador for YouTube's Creators For Change campaign.

Follow Humza on Twitter, Snapchat and Instagram @HumzaProduction and on YouTube @HumzaProductions

HENRY WHITE is a comedy writer working in television and children's fiction. He grew up in west London and began his career in online animation. Henry went on to write and direct adverts for a number of British comedy channels, before working as a sitcom writer. He has a birthmark shaped like a duck.

CHAPTER ONE
A BEE NAMED MUSTAFA

You've probably heard of me, right? Little Badman. No? Oh. Well. . . Doesn't matter. You will do one day. I'm gonna be big. And not like my Uncle Abdul, who ate his own bodyweight in samosas and ended up in hospital. The good kind of big. Rich, famous and respected. Like Jay–Z, or that old white man from KFC.

I was always destined to be big. Even when I was born my mum said it was like trying to fit a nappy on a dishwasher. I call it big boned. Whatever. Point is, I'm a big fish in a small pond. Like a shark in a fish bowl, or a pit bull in a hamster cage. Sooner or later, I'm gonna explode out of there and the world is gonna know my name. Humza Khan.

But you can call me Little Badman.

My path to greatness wasn't always clear. Even a ninja-rapper-gangster like me has to start somewhere. And I started in the hood. Proper gangland territory: the Little Meadows Primary School, Eggington. To say there was a lot of gun crime would be an understatement. There was loads. Just not in Eggington. Mostly in America, I think. Still, I reckon it shaped me into the twelve-year-old I am today.

But nothing, and I mean nothing, shaped me as much as my final year at primary school. I don't know if you've ever seen any war movies, about Vietnam or Iraq or the Galactic Empire, but none of that compares to what I went through in my final year at school. To call myself the greatest hero the world has ever known would be arrogant, so I won't do that. I'll leave you all to form your own opinion once you get to the end of my tale.

And, like so many of history's greatest conflicts, it all began with something so small. In my case, it was a bee named Mustafa . . .

I was sitting in class next to Umer, when his pencil case started to vibrate.

'Is it me or is your pencil case ringing?' I asked, watching the little metal box rattle along the desk.

'Nah, that's just my bee,' replied Umer. 'He's always doing that.'

'Why've you got a bee in your pencil case, man? Let that bee go!'

'No way,' Umer said, trying carefully to peer inside the lid without the bee escaping. 'I'm keeping him. I've never had a pet before.'

'A bee ain't a pet. You can't stroke a bee or teach it tricks. A bee's a bee.'

'Doesn't mean it can't be a pet,' said Umer. 'My cousin had a worm named Liam.'

'Yeah, well, at least a worm ain't gonna sting you.'

'Mustafa wouldn't sting me.'

'Who the hell is Mustafa?'

'My bee,' replied Umer.

'You called your bee Mustafa?'

'Yeah, Mustafa Bee.'

'Why?'

'Because I . . . *must-av-a bee*.'

'I don't even know why we're friends, man.'

See, this is the kind of thing I have to put up with. I'm not saying Umer's an idiot, but you can only watch someone put their shoes on the wrong feet so many times before you start to wonder. Still, he *is* my best friend. Not forever, obviously. When I'm a famous ninja-rapper I'll probably be best friends with Busta Rhymes or Dr Dre, or one of the Power Rangers. But, for now, I've got to put up with Umer.

'Ow!' shouted Umer, slamming the pencil case shut.

'Did you just get stung?' I asked.

'No,' replied Umer, rubbing his swollen thumb. 'Well . . . maybe.'

'Oh great,' I said. 'Now you've killed him.'

'"Killed him"?' gasped Umer, staring at the pencil case containing his bee. 'What are you talking about? I haven't touched him!'

'You don't have to. Once they sting you, that's it – they die.'

'What? I didn't know that!' cried Umer. 'Why did you do it, Mustafa? Why?'

'Quiet down, man – we're gonna get in trouble.'

'Oh, Mustafa! Why?' wailed Umer, tears filling his eyes.

'You two!' came a voice from the front of the class. 'What's going on back there?'

'Uh, nothing, miss,' I replied. 'Umer just got stung by a bee.'

'He's dying, miss! He's dying!' bawled Umer.

'Who's dying?' said Miss Crumble, sounding panicked.

'Mustafa!' replied Umer.

'Who on earth is Mustafa?' asked Miss Crumble, arriving at the desk.

'My bee! My poor dead bee!'

'A bee?' she said, looking a little nervous and taking a step back. 'You're sure he's dead?'

'He's a goner, miss,' I replied. 'Umer basically murdered him.'

'I didn't mean to!' wailed Umer.

'OK, as long as you're certain he's dead,' she said, looking relieved.

'I'm afraid so, miss,' I replied, shaking my head. 'He's buzzed his last buzz. Gone to the great beehive in the sky. He's making honey for Tupac.'

'For goodness' sake,' muttered Miss Crumble. 'It's always something with you two, isn't it?'

'Don't blame me,' I replied. 'Blame Mr Bee-keeper here.'

'Hey, look!' Umer beamed, looking up from the open pencil case. 'He's not dead after all!'

Now it wasn't long after that that I learned some important lessons about bees. Firstly, not all bees die after they sting you – turns out that's just honeybees. Secondly, big hairy Mustafa was actually a bumblebee and had no intention of dying anytime soon. And thirdly (and this one was probably most important of all), Miss Crumble is, and always has been, super allergic to bee-stings. Like crazy, serious, life-threatening allergic. Oops.

Miss Crumble let out a scream so loud and horrible that Wendy Wang's glasses shattered right there on her face. Miss C began to flail her arms around like a windmill in a hurricane, desperately trying to swat poor Mustafa.

'Calm down, miss,' I said. 'It's only a bee.'

But Miss Crumble wasn't listening. She was in a wild panic. No one in the class was laughing, because none of us could decide if this was hilarious or actually a bit scary. I mean, seriously, she looked insane. She was knocking over desks, pulling posters off the walls, spinning around so fast I felt dizzy just watching her. And then the inevitable happened. You can only imprison an innocent bee for so long before he cracks. And Mustafa had had enough.

Flying between Miss Crumble's windmilling fists, Mustafa scored a direct hit, right on the end of her nose. Pow! You could almost hear the sting popping into that big red veiny target. Miss Crumble froze instantly. She stopped screaming, stopped swinging her arms. She just looked at the end of her nose until she went fully cross-eyed. Mustafa looked right back at her. He wiggled his bum, gave a short victorious buzz and then flew out the window.

'Bye, Mustafa,' said Umer, waving. 'I'll never forget you.'

Miss Crumble still didn't move an inch – except for her nose, which was already growing at an alarming rate. It was like someone was inflating a balloon in there. In an instant the swelling had spread to her cheeks, her neck, her hands.

She plonked down in her chair, looking dazed.

'Mnnnggg nugg unggg,' she said, which I think roughly translates as: *my tongue has swollen.*

'Huh,' I said, watching her slowly inflate. 'Do you reckon she's gonna burst?'

'I hope not,' replied Umer. 'Maybe we should go get some help?'

'I dunno. She's had a pretty good innings.'

'Humza!'

'Yeah, yeah, OK,' I said, pushing my seat out. 'I mean, if you felt that bad about killing a bee, imagine how you're gonna feel after killing a teacher.'

'Humza!' cried Umer, who was starting to look a bit ill himself.

'Only playing, man. Come on – let's go save the day.'

And with that we jumped up and ran off to look for a teacher who wasn't about to explode.

When the ambulance took her away, Miss Crumble looked like a beach ball dressed as a woman. I couldn't help but feel like maybe I was just a tiny little bit responsible. After all, I was the one who had assured her Mustafa was dead. But, in my defence, if there are gaps in my knowledge about bees, who could be more responsible than my own teacher? So really, when you take that into account, it was all Miss Crumble's fault and I'm totally blameless. I felt much better after that.

'Come on, Umer,' I said. 'Let's go shoot some more scenes for the video.'

'I don't know, Humza. Aren't we meant to be in a lesson?'

'How we gonna go to a lesson when the teacher's dead?'

'Dead?' said Umer, looking shocked.

'Or sick, I don't know. I ain't a doctor. Now come on – if we're quick, we can film the whole chorus before lunch.'

'Not so fast, you two,' came a booming voice from nearby.

'Uh-oh,' said Umer, swallowing so hard you could hear it.

Before we could even turn round, a large hairy hand fell on each of our shoulders.

'What's this I hear about you two and Miss Crumble?' asked Mr Offalbox.

Now I don't know what your headmaster's like, but ours was big. King Kong big. Like a Volvo in a tie. Have you ever seen one of those cop shows on TV where there's a really angry sergeant? Well, ours looked like the sergeant that ate that sergeant. He had this huge moustache, like the head of a broom, that stretched and contracted like a caterpillar when he spoke. His head alone must have weighed the same as my sofa. He was not someone you wanted to get on the wrong side of.

'Uh, I can explain!' I said as fast as I could get the words out.

'No need for that, Humza,' said Mr Offalbox. 'The paramedics explained everything.'

Uh-oh. I had a sinking feeling I was about to get it, and get it bad. And, however bad Mr Offalbox could be, it wouldn't come close to the trouble I'd be in when my mum and dad found out. No one punishes like a Pakistani parent. They take courses in it. Evening classes on the subject of making their kids suffer. So, at this point, I figured I might just have to run away and join the circus. Or the Mafia. Whichever was easier to get into. And then something unexpected happened.

'You boys are heroes!' said Mr Offalbox. 'They

say that without your quick thinking Miss Crumble might well have died. Well done, the pair of you!'

'Oh, right,' I said with a smile. 'Yeah, I was about to say the same thing.'

'Did they explain about Mustafa?' asked Umer, before I could elbow him in the ribs.

'*Shut up about Mustafa!*' I hissed, then added a little louder: 'What he means is, did they mention that we *must-have-a* reward for our bravery?'

'Well, no, they didn't,' said Mr Offalbox. 'But, now you mention it, I think that's a very good idea.'

'How about half a day off for good behaviour?' I suggested.

'HA HA HA!' roared Mr Offalbox, leaning back with his hands on his hips. 'Of course not! But I think I might just be able to convince the dinner ladies to give you a second helping of dessert.'

'Yeah, good luck with that,' I replied. 'Those old girls are strict as. Have you even seen the healthy stuff they make us eat these days? I swear I'm turning into a rabbit.'

'Just you leave it to me, Humza. I know a thing or two about charming dinner ladies,' he said with a wink, and turned to walk away.

'Urgh,' I said to Umer after he'd gone. 'Old

people shouldn't wink. I just swallowed some sick.'

'Still, double dessert. That's not a bad result,' he replied.

'Yeah, maybe we should nearly kill teachers more often!'

'Hmm, I don't know. One's probably enough for me.'

'Fair enough. Come on, then – let's go film that shot.'

See, school is just a place I go to every day. Sort of like prison, but with worse food. My *real* work is making the greatest rap music video ever produced. How else am I expected to become so famous that people fight wars over me? I'm gonna be so big Little Badman Impersonator will be a valid career choice. I'm gonna be so popular that cats'll learn to speak just to ask me for selfies. I'm gonna be so rich that even my butler's butler will have a butler. And the only way to do any of that is to make myself a smash-hit music video. Enter my cameraman, Umer.

Now, Umer may not have a lot of media training, and he might be shooting on his dad's old Nokia from the Stone Age, and he may shake quite a lot when he's nervous, but, all of that aside, he's got a pretty good eye. And, more importantly, he's the only one I can get to do the job. But it shouldn't matter too much – after all, when you're pointing the camera at me, it's hard to go wrong.

'Uh, Humza,' said Umer ten minutes later, while looking through the tiny screen on his phone. 'I don't know how gangsta this feels.'

'What do you mean?'

'Well . . . it kind of looks like you're in a toilet. At a primary school.'

'Really? How can you tell?'

'Probably the little urinals. They're a bit of a giveaway.'

'Hmm. That ain't ideal. But it's the best we're gonna do. Can you frame them out?'

'Maybe, but I'm trying not to show too much of the graffiti.'

'Why? We did that specially.'

'Well, it's just that it doesn't look very real. You can tell we've done it on paper and stuck it to the walls.'

'Of course we have. We don't want to get in trouble, do we?' I said.

'Yeah, no, of course. But, you know, that's the bit that's not very gangsta.'

'I see what you're saying. Real rappers don't worry about getting detention. OK, just show a bit of the toilets and a bit of the graffiti. People are mostly gonna be looking at me anyway.'

'Got it,' said Umer, and hit RECORD.

I took a deep breath and pulled my best gangsta face (basically you just squint a little and look like you've never smiled for a photo in your life). Then I started spitting my rhymes:

**'B to the A to the D to the Man,
If other rappers can't, Little Badman can.
Straight from the hood like a rat from a drain,
Rhymes so sick they're melting your brain.'**

14

That was as far as I got before the door to the toilet burst open.

'There you are!' snarled Mr Offalbox. Even with just his head peering round the door he seemed huge. Maybe the tiny urinals added to the illusion. It looked like the giant in Jack and the Beanstalk had stopped by for a wee. We had nowhere to run. And that was when I spotted her: Wendy Wang, peering round the door beside the headmaster. Of course! Classic Wendy Wang. She just couldn't keep it to herself.

'Wendy here says,' began Mr Offalbox, 'that perhaps you two aren't the heroes I took you for. Is that so?'

'Define "heroes",' I replied.

'She says it was you two who got Miss Crumble stung in the first place, that you'd been tormenting that bee and then lied about it being deceased.'

'How would Wendy Wang know? She hasn't even got her glasses on.'

'That's your fault too!' said Wendy, before hiding a little further behind the door.

'Humza, imagine you were me,' continued Mr Offalbox.

'I don't know if my imagination's big enough, sir,' I replied.

'Shut up, boy,' he muttered. 'Now, if you were me and you received one side of a story from top student, class president and chess-team captain Wendy Wang, and a very different, contradictory story from D-student, class clown and boy voted most likely to get caught in a bear trap Humza Khan, who would *you* believe?'

'Definitely the bear-trap guy. He sounds pretty honest.'

'Well then, that's where you and I differ,' said Mr Offalbox, with narrowing eyes.

'Does this mean we're not getting our extra pudding?' asked Umer.

'The only "extra" you're getting is an hour's extra detention after school.'

'Ah, man! That ain't fair!' I said. 'It wasn't on purpose!'

'Isn't that always your excuse, Humza?' said Mr Offalbox.

'No. I've got lots of excuses. I once said a ghost broke the canteen window.'

'And did anyone believe you?'

'No.'

'And no one believes you now. So, unless you want detention every day this week, get out of this toilet immediately and take that ridiculous graffiti with you. I'll be teaching your lessons for the rest of the day. And I'm in the mood for extra homework.'

Man, Offalbox had to be the worst headmaster in the world! We used to have this nice old woman named Mrs Prume, who was pretty easy to confuse. I barely ever got caught when she was around. Then Offalbox showed up and suddenly we got detentions, extra homework, lines . . . I tell you, that ain't acceptable at primary school! How was I meant to enjoy misbehaving if I kept getting punished for it?

It was already getting dark when Umer and I got out of school. I was dragging my feet because I knew I'd be in trouble when I got home. My mum would ask me why I was late and, if I lied, she'd work it out. So I'd have to tell her the truth, and then she'd tell my dad, and then he'd threaten me with some weird punishment I've never heard of before, like a two-hour headstand or sleeping in a drawer.

Umer was looking at his phone and the screen was lighting up his face in the darkness.

'Hmm,' he said after a while. 'I'm not sure this is going to work after all.'

'What?' I asked.

He turned the phone screen to show me the footage we'd shot earlier. At least that's what I think it was. A blocky brown thing was moving near some blocky white things.

'What the hell is that, man?' I asked.

'You're the blocky brown thing,' said Umer helpfully.

'I figured that. But you can't even tell I'm handsome! Hell, you can't even tell I'm human!'

'Well, on the plus side, at least you can't tell it's a toilet either.'

'You can't tell anything! This is terrible! How old is that phone?'

'About twice as old as us,' replied Umer.

'Ah, man, this is never gonna work. Why can't you have a proper phone?'

'It's the only phone my dad will give me. Can we use yours?'

'You know I've only got a pager,' I snapped.

'What's a pager?'

I showed him the little black box my dad had given me.

'It's like a phone that only accepts text messages,' I said. 'Doctors have 'em. I think it's three times as old as we are.'

'Does it have a video camera?'

'Take a wild guess.'

'Well then, I don't know how we're going to make your music video, Humza.'

'But I've got to make it, man! How else am I gonna take over the world and leave all you suckers behind?'

'You could study hard and gain qualifications in an area you find rewarding?' suggested Umer.

'Yeah, or I could catch a leprechaun and make him grant me wishes, but both those ideas are fantasy. I've got to make this video, Umer! I've just got to!'

And that was when I saw it. We'd come to a stop outside the shops on the high street and, at first, neither of us had noticed the window display. When Umer saw me staring open-mouthed, he turned to look. Right there in the centre of the window was the most beautiful thing I had ever seen. The Matsani S3000 Home Pro Compact Video Camera. White moulded plastic with sharp black outlining. Optical zoom lens. 16-megapixel sensor. Three-inch fold-out LCD screen. And all this in a package roughly the size of a chihuahua's head. I had to have it.

'That'd do the job,' said Umer.

'That *will* do the job,' I replied.

'Really? How? It's £150.'

'Yeah, but it's marked down from £300.'

'OK, but that's still £150 more than you've got.'

'Doesn't matter,' I replied, staring at the twinkling lens in the display case. 'It's destiny, Umer. It *will* be mine . . . Oh yes . . . It *will* be mine!'

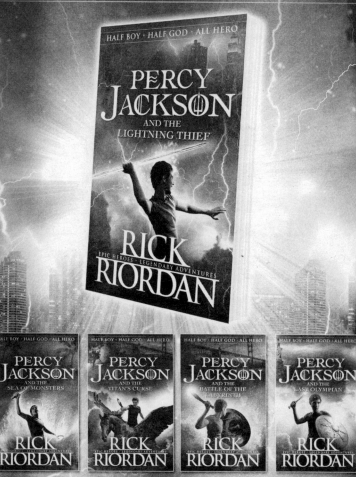

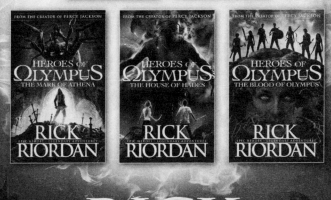

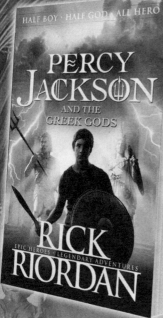

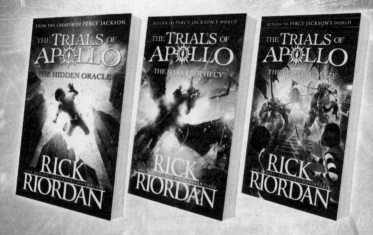

EXPERIENCE RICK RIORDAN'S WORLD IN A WHOLE NEW WAY WITH THESE INCREDIBLE GRAPHIC NOVELS

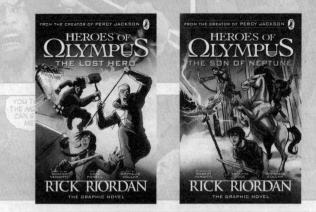

THE ADVENTURE NEVER STOPS . . .

PERCY JACKSON

THE GREEK GODS ARE ALIVE AND KICKING!

They still fall in love with mortals and bear children with immortal blood in their veins. When Percy Jackson learns he's the son of Poseidon, god of the sea, he must travel to Camp Half-Blood – a secret base dedicated to the training of young demigods.

PERCY JACKSON AND THE LIGHTNING THIEF
PERCY JACKSON AND THE SEA OF MONSTERS
PERCY JACKSON AND THE TITAN'S CURSE
PERCY JACKSON AND THE BATTLE OF THE LABYRINTH
PERCY JACKSON AND THE LAST OLYMPIAN

THE DEMIGOD FILES
CAMP HALF-BLOOD CONFIDENTIAL

PERCY JACKSON AND THE GREEK GODS
PERCY JACKSON AND THE GREEK HEROES

HEROES OF OLYMPUS

PERCY JACKSON IS BACK!

Percy and his old friends from Camp Half-Blood join forces with new Roman demigods from Camp Jupiter for a deadly new mission: to prevent the all-powerful Earth Mother, Gaia, from awakening from her millennia-long sleep to bring about the end of the world.

THE LOST HERO
THE SON OF NEPTUNE
THE MARK OF ATHENA
THE HOUSE OF HADES
THE BLOOD OF OLYMPUS

THE DEMIGOD DIARIES

THE TRIALS OF APOLLO

AN OLYMPIAN HAS FALLEN!

The god Apollo has been cast down from Olympus in the body of a teenage boy.
With the help of friends like Percy Jackson and familiar faces from
Camp Half-Blood, he must complete a series of harrowing trials to save
the world from a dangerous new enemy.

THE HIDDEN ORACLE
THE DARK PROPHECY
THE BURNING MAZE

THE GODS OF EGYPT AWAKEN!

When an explosion shatters the ancient Rosetta Stone and unleashes Set, the
Egyptian god of chaos, only Carter and Sadie Kane can save the day. Their quest
takes the pair around the globe in a battle against the gods of Ancient Egypt.

THE RED PYRAMID
THE THRONE OF FIRE
THE SERPENT'S SHADOW

BROOKLYN HOUSE MAGICIAN'S MANUAL

THE GODS OF ASGARD ARISE!

After being killed in battle with a fire giant, Magnus Chase finds himself
resurrected in Valhalla as one of the chosen warriors of the Norse god Odin.
The gods of Asgard are preparing for Ragnarok – the Norse doomsday –
and Magnus has a leading role . . .

MAGNUS CHASE AND THE SWORD OF SUMMER
MAGNUS CHASE AND THE HAMMER OF THOR
MAGNUS CHASE AND THE SHIP OF THE DEAD

9 FROM THE NINE WORLDS
HOTEL VALHALLA GUIDE TO THE NORSE WORLDS

WORLD
BOOK
DAY

SHARE A STORY

Well **hello** there! We are

Overjoyed that you have **joined our celebration** of

Reading books and **sharing stories**, because we

Love bringing **books** to you.

Did you know, we are a **charity** dedicated to celebrating the

Brilliance of **reading for pleasure** for everyone, everywhere?

Our mission is to help you discover **brand new stories** and

Open your mind to exciting **new worlds** and **characters**, from

Kings and **queens** to **wizards** and **pirates** to **animals** and **adventurers** and so many more. We couldn't

Do it without all the amazing **authors** and **illustrators**, **booksellers** and **bookshops**, publishers, schools and **libraries** out there –

And most importantly, we couldn't do it all without . . .

YOU!

On your bookmarks, get set, READ!
Happy Reading. Happy World Book Day.

WORLD BOOK DAY

SHARE A STORY

From breakfast to bedtime, there's always time to discover and share stories together. You can . . .

1 TAKE A TRIP to your **LOCAL BOOKSHOP**

Brimming with brilliant books and helpful booksellers to share awesome reading recommendations, you can also enjoy booky events with your favourite authors and illustrators.

 FIND YOUR LOCAL BOOKSHOP: booksellers.org.uk/ bookshopsearch

2 JOIN your **LOCAL LIBRARY**

That wonderful place where the hugest selection of books you could ever want to read awaits – and you can borrow them for FREE! Plus expert advice and fantastic free family reading events.

 FIND YOUR LOCAL LIBRARY: findmylibrary.co.uk

3 CHECK OUT the **WORLD BOOK DAY WEBSITE**

Looking for reading tips, advice and inspiration? There is so much for you to discover at **worldbookday.com**, packed with fun activities, games, downloads, podcasts, videos, competitions and all the latest new books galore.

SPONSORED BY

NATIONAL BOOK tokens

Illustrations © Rob Biddulph

Celebrate stories. Love reading.

World Book Day is a registered charity.